RODNEY TO
THE RESCUE

1018548

ROBOTS™

RODNEY TO THE RESCUE

Written by Kathleen W. Zoehfeld

HarperKidsEntertainment
An Imprint of HarperCollins*Publishers*

CHAPTER ONE

Growing Up
in Rivet Town

"Waaaaahhh!" A baby's cry filled the room. Mr. and Mrs. Copperbottom looked at their child lovingly.

"Twelve hours of labor. Oh, but it was worth it." Mrs. Copperbottom sighed.

The baby robot they had just built from a Build-a-Baby kit smiled up at them sweetly.

Mr. Copperbottom took his son in his arms. "Look at him! Rodney Copperbottom. Look at how bright his eyes are! Oh, honey, I don't know how I'm going to do it, but somehow I'm going to see that he has everything he needs."

Life in Rivet Town was not easy for the Copperbottoms. When little Rodney's birthdays came around, he never got shiny new parts like the other robots. His big-boy parts were a hodgepodge of hand-me-downs with chipped paint and leaky joints.

Mr. Copperbottom washed dishes for Mr. Gunk, the owner of the local restaurant. As a kid, Mr. Copperbottom had dreamed of being a musician. But his own parts didn't include any fancy horns or strings for making music. Instead, he had a dishwasher fitted right in the middle of his chest.

Even though he brought extra work home every evening, Mr. Copperbottom barely made enough money to make ends meet.

By the time Rodney had his grown-up parts attached, he was working at the restaurant, too. But Rodney's real dream was to be an inventor, just like his hero, Bigweld.

Every week without fail, he and his dad watched their favorite TV program, *The Bigweld Show*, together. Bigweld ran the biggest, brightest factory in Robot City.

"Every day robots come here from hither and yon, bringing us new ideas," said Bigweld. "And I listen to every single one of 'em, because you never know which young bot is going to change the world. Remember, whether a bot is made of new parts, old parts, or spare parts—you can shine no matter what you're made of."

"He's talking to me, Dad," cried Rodney.

"He sure is, son!" cheered his dad. "He sure is!"

"You know, I love to tinker." Rodney heard his hero say. "But why invent anything unless it makes someone's life better? See a need, fill a need!"

"That's it! I have to look for a need," said Rodney. He looked for his dad's reaction, but the weary Mr. Copperbottom was already fast asleep.

Evening after evening, Rodney tinkered in his room, trying to develop a new bot that could help overworked robots like his dad.

Finally his invention was ready! He called it the Wonderbot. Rodney brought it to the restaurant where he and his dad worked.

"Yeah! Wow!" shouted the kitchen crew as the bot

began loading, removing, drying, and stacking dishes all at once.

"What *is* that?" shouted Mr. Gunk.

"My son invented it," said Mr. Copperbottom proudly.

"What's it doing?" boomed Gunk.

"Mr. Gunk, please, you're making it nervous," pleaded Rodney.

The Wonderbot began to shake with fear. Then it started bouncing uncontrollably around the kitchen, smashing plates and breaking bowls.

"Clean up this mess!" Mr. Gunk commanded Mr. Copperbottom.

"And *you*," he shouted, pointing to Rodney, "get out! Inventor . . . ha! You're the son of a dishwasher, and that's all you'll ever be."

CHAPTER TWO

Robot City

Rodney knew that it was time to make a change. It was clear to him that he needed to go to Robot City and meet his hero Bigweld. He wanted to get a job and help his dad pay back Mr. Gunk.

"I'm never gonna be someone here," Rodney complained to his parents. "I want to be an inventor. I want to *be* somebody."

Rodney's mom hugged him tight. She dried her tears and waved good-bye as he boarded the train.

"I won't let you down, Dad," Rodney cried. "I'll make you proud!"

Robot City was dazzling! Bots of all types rushed this way and that. Rodney rode the Ferris wheel–like escalator to the amazing Bigweld Express.

But when he arrived at the front gates of Bigweld Industries, he found that things were very different from what he expected.

Tim, the gate guard, was on duty.

"I'd like to see Mr. Bigweld," Rodney said. "*I'm* an inventor!"

"Sorry, kid. Nobody gets in. Company rules," said Tim.

"Company rules?" asked Rodney. "Well then, how do they hire new inventors?"

"They don't. Those days are over. My advice? Come back two years ago," Tim said, laughing at his own joke.

Rodney stalked away. "I'll be back! You can't stop me!"

"Sure I can," sneered Tim. "Those are my orders: 'Keep out the losers!'"

"I'm not a loser!" cried Rodney.

"No? Well if you were a winner, you'd be up there

with the big shots." Tim pointed to the windows of the boardroom, high atop the building.

Rodney didn't know it yet, but in that boardroom Phineas T. Ratchet, the new head of Bigweld Industries, was busy undoing everything Bigweld stood for.

Ratchet glowered at his executives. "What's our big-ticket item? Upgrades, people. Upgrades! Now, if we're telling robots that no matter what they're made of, they're fine, how can we expect them to feel *crummy* enough about themselves to buy our upgrades and make themselves look better? Am I right?"

The executives cringed. "Right. Of course he's right. . . ."

"Therefore I've come up with a new slogan: 'Why Be *You*, When You Can Be *New*?'"

"Oooo, wonderful!" everyone agreed.

Everyone, that is, except a beautiful young executive named Cappy who still believed in Bigweld's kind ideals. "Why would robots buy new upgrades if spare parts are so much cheaper?" she asked.

"Well, that's easy," explained Ratchet as he angrily knocked boxes of spare parts from the table, "because as of today we are no longer *making* spare parts."

Meanwhile, Rodney had figured out a way in. The Wonderbot had flown him up to the roof. While Ratchet was finishing his speech, Rodney dropped through a skylight, tumbled onto the conference table, and slid right into Cappy's lap!

Rodney had never seen such a pretty bot before. He struggled to collect himself.

"Sir," he said, turning to Ratchet. "I am a young inventor. And it's always been my dream to come to Robot City and present my ideas to Mr. Bigweld . . . who doesn't seem to be here."

"Gee, no. But while he's away he left me in charge," snarled Ratchet.

"Oh, well then, let me show *you* what my Wonderbot can do," tried Rodney.

"I have a better idea," snapped Ratchet. "Why don't you let *me* show *you* what it can do." He snatched the Wonderbot and kicked it out the window.

"No!" cried Cappy.

Before he knew it, Rodney was being hoisted up by the magnet on a security crane and flung back outside the gates.

CHAPTER THREE

The Rusties

Magnetized by the crane, Rodney began attracting junk. Nuts, bolts, scrap metal, garbage cans—everything came flying toward him and stuck to him as he stormed away from Bigweld Industries.

Clank! An oxygen tank fell into his path and tripped him. Rodney skidded and sparks flew. *Kaboom!* The oxygen exploded, sending Rodney rocketing down the street and into a garbage can, where he lay, dented and unconscious.

As Rodney came to, he felt a strange tugging sensation in his foot, and he heard someone singing, "I'm a little teapot, short and stout."

The singing bot was removing one of Rodney's feet!

"Hey!" shouted Rodney.

The bot ran.

"Hey, you've got my foot!"

The bot bumped into a stack of cans filled with ball bearings. They came down around them like hail and scattered all over the ground. Rodney tried to grab his stolen foot, and he and the bot slid around like a couple of ice dancers.

The bot pulled away and crashed against a wall. *Kablam!* "Ow!" His head fell off and hit the floor. "Oh, great. Happy now?" asked the head.

"Not until you give me back my foot, you mugger," Rodney yelled. He yanked his foot away from the bot's headless body.

"I'm not a mugger! My name's Fender. And I happen to be a *scrounger.*"

Rodney reattached his own foot. Then he offered to help Fender reattach his head.

"No, no, I'll do it myself," said the head. "I have my pride, you know."

As Fender's body groped around trying to find his head, he accidentally kicked it farther and farther away. His head bounced into a Dumpster full of scrap metal. Nearby, his friends, Lug, Crank Casey, Diesel

Springer, and Fender's sister, Piper Pinwheeler, were looking for spare parts. They were scroungers, too, and they called themselves "the Rusties."

"Hey, check *this* out," cried Piper, picking up Rodney's Wonderbot.

"Owww!" cried Fender's head as his body crashed down into the Dumpster on top of it.

Piper looked into the cart and sighed, "Fender, what happened to you *now*?"

Rodney pointed at his Wonderbot. "Hey, that's mine!" he shouted.

"That's him!" cried Fender. "He knocked my head off!"

"All right, buster!" Piper scowled at him. "Hey, you're kind of cute."

"Piper, would you behave yourself," said Crank. "Now come on. Let's get Fender fixed."

Piper handed Rodney the Wonderbot. "See ya around," she said.

The Rusties led Fender to Jack Hammer's Hardware Store. But when they got there, Jack told them there

were no more spare parts, only upgrades. Fender was officially outmoded. Fender panicked, "How could this happen to me? I'm practically a kid!"

"Sorry, pal. It's either upgrade or the Chop Shop for you," said Jack.

The Rusties started to worry until Piper spoke up. "No one's going to the Chop Shop. We are not junk. We are not scrap. And we will not be treated this way."

CHAPTER FOUR

Aunt Fan's Boarding House

The Rusties were struggling to find a way to reattach Fender's head when they heard a familiar voice.

"I can fix you easy," said Rodney.

Piper leaned in and watched him begin working.

"Hold still, this might tickle," Rodney told Fender. He turned Fender's head upside down and tightened a bolt.

The Rusties decided if Rodney could fix Fender, he was probably an okay guy. They asked him why he'd ended up in a garbage can. Rodney told them how he had tried to talk to Bigweld.

The Rusties scoffed.

"Bigweld's gone." Piper sighed. "It's like there never was a Bigweld."

"Of course there's a Bigweld," said Rodney.

"What I heard is that they have done him in," said Crank. "And they left the rest of us to fall apart. That's why there's no part for Fender's neck."

"And when you *totally* fall apart, you become sweeper bait," added Fender.

At that moment, a sweeper came down the road, making awful chomping noises. Sweepers were powerful machines that scooped up spare parts and crushed them into scrap metal.

"Ew! Those things give me the creeps," cried Crank.

Fender pointed to his neck impatiently.

"Well, that ought to do it," said Rodney.

Fender spun his head around in glee. "Hey, look at that! He fixed my neck!! Here's one outmode you're not gonna get!" he cried, taunting the sweeper. He wagged his butt. It fell off and hit the street with a clank.

The Rusties had no idea how much danger they were in! The sweeper was on its way to a warehouse where the evil Madame Gasket had set up a giant

Chop Shop. She and her minions were busy melting down all the spare parts in town to make the new metal upgrades for Bigweld Industries.

But it wasn't only spare parts that were getting gobbled up by her sweepers. Although the Rusties didn't know it, Ratchet was Madame Gasket's son. He needed more metal, and she was going to provide it—even if it meant sweeping live outmodes right off the streets! Not only that, she was planning to get rid of Bigweld once and for all.

With a little luck, the Rusties made it home to Aunt Fan's safe and sound. Fender opened the door and invited Rodney in. "When in Robot City, guests of the Rusties stay at Aunt Fan's Boarding House," he declared.

"Are you sure your aunt won't mind?" asked Rodney.

Aunt Fan was a kind bot who took in bots that were down on their luck. She wasn't actually anyone's aunt, but once Rodney saw her huge fanny, and was nearly

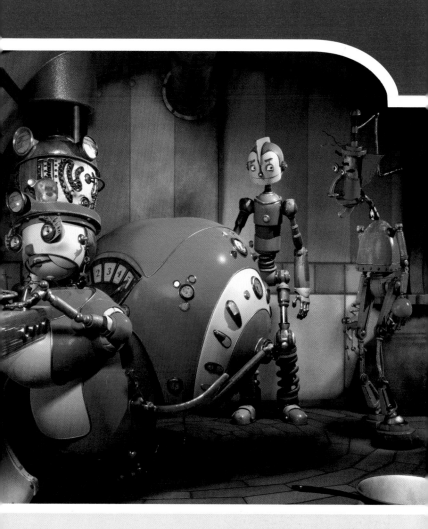

knocked over by it, he understood how she got her name. She told Rodney to make himself at home.

"Thank you, that's very kind," said Rodney.

"My pleasure," replied Aunt Fan. "See a need, fill a need."

"Hey, just like Bigweld," said Rodney. Bigweld was Aunt Fan's hero, too!

The next morning at breakfast, Aunt Fan served everyone some of her special fresh-brewed grease. Rodney was grateful to have a cozy place to spend the night and share meals, but it didn't ease all his worries.

"What are you guys doing today?" he asked.

"We're doing it," replied Fender.

"Mr. Bigweld's disappeared and you're just gonna sit here!?" cried Rodney. "It's wrong! There should be rioting in the streets!!"

Suddenly, they heard robots screaming. Rodney and the Rusties jumped up and hurried outside. A crowd of bots was running down the street in a panic!

CHAPTER FIVE

Rodney Sees a Need

The nervous robots gathered outside Jack Hammer's Hardware Store shouting: "Parts! Parts! We want parts!"

"Sorry, folks," shouted Jack, "nothing but upgrades from here on in." At that moment a truck marked UPGRADES came rumbling by. It had a big picture of Ratchet on the side.

When Rodney and the Rusties raced up, someone pointed at Rodney and cried, "Hey, look! Isn't that the guy who fixed Fender's neck?"

Rodney was famous! The frantic crowd surged around him, pleading with him for help. There were broken arms and eyes and butts. Everyone needed something different. Rodney was overwhelmed.

"Back off!" cried Fender, trying to shield Rodney from the mob.

29

Rodney focused on the truck with Ratchet's picture on it. Suddenly he got a determined look in his eye. "See a need, fill a need," he said to himself.

The next thing the crowd knew, Rodney had set up

shop and began doing whatever repairs he could, all with the help of the Rusties.

Meanwhile, down at the Chop Shop, Ratchet paid

a visit to his mother to let her know that soon there would be plenty of scrap metal and no more outmodes.

"Such a good boy . . . And after you finish off Bigweld, there will be nobody out there to fix them."

"That wasn't part of the plan," Ratchet cried. But his mother convinced him that they needed to get rid of Bigweld if they wanted their dreams of running Robot City to come true.

Back at Aunt Fan's house, Rodney was running out of materials and out of ideas. The line of needy bots seemed to stretch for miles. "The only way to solve this problem is to find Bigweld!" Rodney told the Rusties.

The Wonderbot got their attention. He unrolled a fancy poster that announced: BIGWELD BALL TONIGHT.

"Of course!" exclaimed Aunt Fan. "I'm sure he'll go to that!"

"Well that's it then," declared Rodney. "I'm going to the Bigweld Ball!"

CHAPTER SIX

Crashing the Party

Of course outmodes like Rodney were not invited to the gala event. Tim, the security guard, was posted at the door, making sure no unwanted bots slipped in.

"Can I help you?" he scowled as Rodney and Fender arrived.

Rodney had created his own shiny new upgrade disguise.

Fender, wearing a dramatic cape, stepped forward and declared, "This is Count Roderick von Brokenzipper!"

Tim scanned the invitation list.

"Where are the trumpets to announce our arrival!?" demanded Fender.

"The, wha—? Um, you're not on the list," Tim stammered.

Fender gasped. "Fine! We will go! You will explain to your superiors why the Count was not able to attend their little luau, their barn dance, whatever this is. We are leaving in a huff!"

"No, no," insisted Tim nervously. "Please—go right in!"

"Fender, that was brilliant," whispered Rodney.

Fender tipped his hat, and the Wonderbot flew out.

"Let's split up," said Rodney. "If you see Bigweld, come find me. If anything goes wrong, we'll signal each other."

Across the room, the dastardly Ratchet was flirting with Cappy. He tossed a cracker in the air and caught it in his mouth, trying to impress her. But when he began to choke on it, she took the opportunity to flee.

She bumped into Rodney in the crowd. "Hey, I know you!" she said. "You're the flying kid."

"I am? . . . I mean, uh . . ." stammered Rodney, speechless and afraid she might give him away.

"Yoo-hoo! Cappy!?" Ratchet called.

"Dance with me!" Cappy ordered Rodney, swooping him out of Ratchet's sight.

Once he recovered his balance, Rodney found himself enjoying the dance. He began searching the room for Bigweld.

Then he heard the host of the gala announcing the big moment: "Ladies and gentlebots, please direct your attention to the stage. . . ."

"Bigweld!" cried Rodney.

But instead of Bigweld, the host announced: "Phineas T. Ratchet!"

Bigweld, it seemed, was unable to attend.

"Not coming?" cried Rodney. "He *has* to come!"

"What? Do you want your money back?" Ratchet sneered.

Rodney mustered his courage. "I came here to see Bigweld."

"Security," snapped Ratchet. "We have a party crasher."

"That's right," declared Rodney, pulling off his disguise. "I had to put all this junk on in order to get in here, so I could tell Bigweld that you are outmoding millions of bots. I know because I spent all day long fixing them!"

In an instant Ratchet recognized the troublesome bot from the boardroom. *"You!"* he boomed.

Rodney signaled frantically for Fender.

Ratchet pulled a security guard aside. "Take him for a drive," he whispered. "And bring me back his exact weight in paper clips."

Cappy overheard him. "No!" she cried.

"No?" asked Ratchet.

"Um . . . I'll show him the door," replied Cappy, thinking fast. She inched up close to Ratchet and smiled at him flirtatiously.

Ratchet hesitated, flustered.

Cappy pushed Rodney and ordered him to get moving.

"What? What are you doing?" asked Rodney.

"Saving your life," she whispered.

"Unhand him!" cried Fender.

Cappy knocked Fender to the floor. "Get out of here, you idiot!"

Rodney quickly introduced her to his pal. Then he grabbed the two of them by their wrists and ran for the door.

Behind them they could hear Ratchet shouting.

Meanwhile, the Wonderbot had started up a conga dance, and Ratchet was stuck in the line! Rodney and his friends were safe, for now.

CHAPTER SEVEN

Bigweld's Mansion

While Fender took off with a pretty bot he'd met at the ball, Rodney and the Wonderbot jumped into Cappy's car.

"That was amazing!" cried Rodney when they were safely out of Ratchet's reach, "the way you just thought of that!"

"Well, you know, that was the most fun I ever had at one of those parties," replied Cappy.

"So, where do we go now?" asked Rodney.

"You're going home," she said.

"No way!" cried Rodney. "Let's go find Bigweld!"

Cappy was worried. If she and Rodney got caught trying to see Bigweld, she could lose everything—her job, her future—and Rodney's life could be in danger.

Rodney was disappointed that Cappy had forgotten

everything Bigweld stood for. "Next time you upgrade yourself, check out the catalog and see if they have a conscience," he said. Cappy thought about what Rodney said and realized that she had to help him find Bigweld.

"Okay, we tried," she said, pulling up in front of Bigweld's mansion. "Nobody's home."

"No, no. Look at all these newspapers and this mail," said Rodney hopefully.

"They probably stopped delivering these years ago," said Cappy.

A newspaper bot came whizzing by and tossed the latest edition in their direction. *Thwak!* It hit Cappy right in the head. There staring up at them was the latest headline: BAD BOT BUSTS BALL.

Rodney had to admit, the place did look deserted. And Ratchet's henchmen were probably out hunting for him right now.

"Come on," cried Cappy. "We gotta get you outta here!"

But Rodney pushed on the huge front door. It creaked open. Cappy reluctantly followed him into the dark hall.

They saw Bigweld's workshop and his amazing inventions. But everything was quiet, as though he'd left right in the middle of a project, never to return.

Suddenly Rodney spotted a row of dominoes lined up on the floor. "Hey, look at this," he cried. "Remember? He used to have these on his show."

Rodney got down on his hands and knees to get a closer look. "But they are so dusty." He blew the dust.

"Wait! Don't!" cried Cappy. "Someone will know we're here."

Too late! The first domino fell. Then the next and the next. There was no stopping them! The toppling domino trail led them to a huge room with rows and rows of more dominoes—a million of them—arranged in a beautiful design. Rodney and Cappy were swept up in their great crashing waves.

Bam! Rodney and Cappy saw a huge figure surf

through the waves and wipe out. It was Bigweld! Cappy and Rodney were speechless.

"Let's set 'em up again," shouted Bigweld. "Only bigger! You start on that end. I'll check back with you in a year."

"Sir, is *this* what you've been working on?" asked Rodney. "*This* is why no one sees you?"

"Nobody likes a chatterbox, young man," he said. He began reassembling his elaborate design.

Rodney couldn't believe his eyes! How could Bigweld be playing like this when there was such a terrible crisis in Robot City?

"Show him that thing you made," suggested Cappy, motioning to the Wonderbot.

"A device? A doohickey? A thingamajig?" Bigweld inquired.

"Yes. I—"

"Not interested."

"But—"

"Oh, all right." Bigweld sighed. "Let's get this over with. Thrill me."

Rodney spoke to the Wonderbot: "Now, don't be scared. Show Mr. Bigweld what you can do." But the poor Wonderbot began shaking, just like it had with Mr. Gunk. It sat quietly for a moment—then exploded!

"Son, let me give you a good piece of advice," said Bigweld. "Give up!"

"What? You're telling me to quit!?" cried Rodney.

"I said give up. But 'quit' works just as well."

"Is that what you did? Is that why you're sitting here letting Ratchet turn robots into outmodes?" asked Rodney.

"Kid, sometimes you've just got to know when you're licked," said Bigweld. "The world got shinier and faster. And I've become . . . an outmode. Ratchet is the future. I'm the past. Go home, kid. If it beat me, it's gonna beat you."

Cappy took Rodney gently by the arm and motioned for them to leave.

"You were right, Cappy," he said glumly. "You can take me to the train station now. Bigweld is dead."

Time to Fight Back!

As Cappy and Rodney waited dejectedly for his train, they heard Aunt Fan calling, "Rodney . . . wait! Don't go yet!" She handed Rodney his suitcase. "The others wanted to see you off, too," she puffed.

She opened the door on her big fanny and Lug, Diesel, Piper, and Crank tumbled out.

Rodney was introducing everyone to Cappy, when they heard Fender's voice shouting, "Hurry! One ticket to *anywhere*!!"

The Rusties stared at him in shock. Even for Fender, he looked pretty weird. He had lost his whole bottom half. And, somehow, he'd scrounged the bottom half of a female bot and attached that instead.

"Fender?" asked Lug in disbelief.

"Guess what!" Fender cried. "It's the sweepers. They're rounding up outmodes and taking them—what

44

them? US!—to Madame Gasket's Chop Shop."

He told them how he'd been swept off the street right after walking his new girlfriend home. He described the whole nightmare—how he'd been taken to the Chop Shop and how he'd fallen apart on the conveyor belt, found a new bottom half, and narrowly escaped being pulverized in the horrible grinder.

"And guess who's really behind it all," he challenged.

"Ratchet!" cried Rodney.

"He's Madame Gasket's son!" exclaimed Fender with a shudder. "It's the end! We won't last a week!"

"Okay. Settle down," said Crank. "I've got a plan. Let's *all* get on that train!!"

"Hey, wait a minute!" cried Rodney. "You're all giving up?"

"You started it," said Crank.

"Well, I'm ending it!" declared Rodney. "We have to fight back!!"

"Fighting never solved anything," said Aunt Fan.

All of a sudden, Bigweld's voice boomed out behind them: "Quitting isn't so productive either."

"It's the big boy!" cried Crank.

"Be still my pump." Aunt Fan sighed.

Bigweld cast her an admiring glance. Then he said to Rodney: "Kid, if you're gonna fight, I'm going in with you."

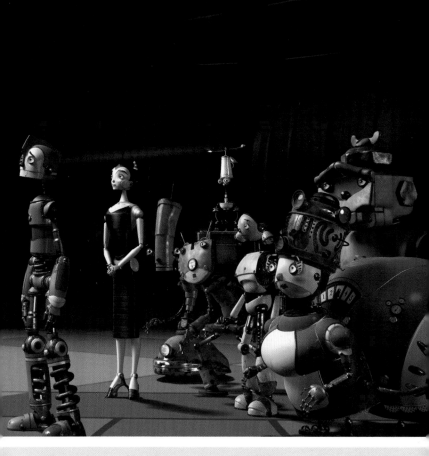

"Then let's do it!" cheered Rodney. They shook hands.

"Come on, gang!" cried Bigweld. "Let's give that Ratchet an old-school fixin'."

The Return of Bigweld

The next morning Bigweld, Rodney, Cappy, and the Rusties piled into Bigweld's limo and drove right up to the door of Bigweld Industries.

Bigweld ordered the Rusties to stay put and watch the limo. Cappy and Rodney were to meet him in the boardroom in ten minutes.

He looked at Cappy. "You know your boyfriend here's a genius."

"Oh, he's not my . . ." she protested. "He is?"

"I am?" asked Rodney.

"Thanks for still believing in me," Bigweld said. He strode off toward the headquarters. "Ahhh, it's good to be home!"

All the executives at Bigweld Industries looked on in amazement as the legendary inventor burst through the doors. "It's Mr. Bigweld!!" they gasped.

Bigweld stormed past them and headed straight for Ratchet's office.

Ratchet was on the phone in a panic, shouting to his assistant. "Tell him I'm not here. Tell him any-thing. . . . Just don't let him walk through that. . . . Ahhhhhhhhhh!"

"Ratchet!" boomed Bigweld. "You're fired!"

"Fired? On what grounds?" protested Ratchet.

Bigweld picked up the phone to call security.

"Wait, please," whimpered Ratchet. "Can I make just one more heartfelt plea?"

"What did you want to say?" asked Bigweld.

Ratchet grabbed the phone and clonked it on Bigweld's head. *"That!"* he cried.

Bigweld fell on the floor, unconscious.

When Rodney and Cappy arrived at the boardroom, they couldn't believe their eyes. Two security guards were holding up a very woozy Bigweld.

"Take fatface to the Chop Shop," Ratchet ordered his guards. "We don't need him anymore." As he turned away, he saw Cappy and Rodney staring at him. He ordered his guards to seize them, too!

But the Wonderbot grabbed the guards and clonked their heads together. Rodney leapt onto Bigweld's shoulders. The Wonderbot attached himself to Bigweld's back and pushed the two of them down the hall.

Crash! They went flying out a window. The Wonderbot tried to set them down gently, but they were too heavy.

"Ahhhhhhhhhhhhh!" Rodney and Bigweld went tumbling down the side of the building.

"Mr. Bigweld," cried Rodney. "Are you okay?"

"Fatface to the Chop Shop! Fatface to the Chop Shop," he chanted in a loopy, singsong voice.

"I'll take that as a no," said Rodney.

Ratchet ran after them shouting, "Get them! Find them! Crush them!"

Wham! Ratchet fell flat on his face. Cappy had stuck out her foot and tripped him.

She hurried down in the elevator and into the lobby. Outside she spotted Rodney and Bigweld bumping down the stairs.

Still waiting in the limo, the Rusties saw Rodney and Bigweld, too—with the security guards close behind them!

Cappy fought off the guards as Rodney and

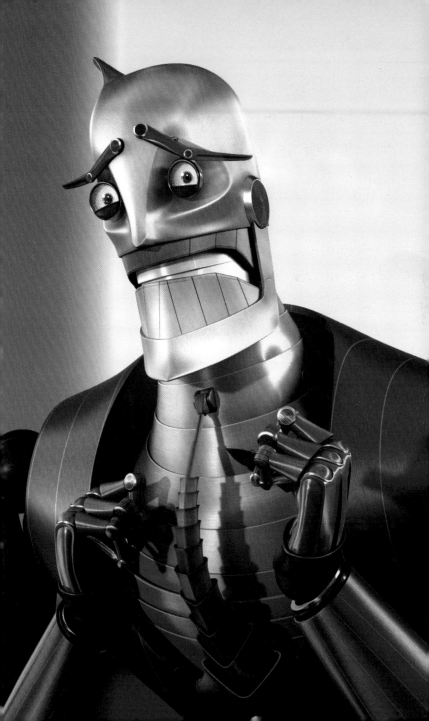

Bigweld escaped out the front gates. She hopped into a security truck with a big magnet crane, and followed.

"Come on! We've gotta help Rodney!" cried Piper.

But Fender wanted to protect his sister and made her and Aunt Fan stay behind. "We're headed for a huge butt-whuppin'," he told them as he sped away in the limo.

Rodney could see two magnet trucks right behind him. He steered Bigweld off the road onto another track. He popped open Bigweld's head and began to repair him as they rolled away.

"Rodney, what's going on? Where are we?" asked Bigweld as he came to.

"It's okay. You're all right," Rodney reassured him.

Clang! Suddenly one of the truck's magnets sucked them right off the track.

"Whoa!" they cried.

They could see Cappy waving to them from the driver's seat!

Clang! Before they had time to cheer, another magnet grabbed them from the other side. It was Ratchet driving the other truck!

Meanwhile, the Rusties had caught up to them in the limo. Lug pushed Fender, Crank, and Diesel up out of the sunroof.

"Ahhhhhhh!" they screamed, as the magnetic forces snapped them up and scrunched them together around Bigweld's body.

Ratchet veered off onto another track, and the Rusties held on for dear life, stretching out between the two magnets like a long tightrope when they were pulled off of Bigweld.

"I've got to pull that plug," cried Rodney. He made his way across the tightrope to Ratchet's truck to demagnetize it. Rodney pulled the plug and all of them went snapping back to Cappy's magnet.

"Hooray!" the Rusties cheered.

But as Cappy turned to look ahead, she saw they were headed straight for the Chop Shop.

"Ahhhhhhhhhhhh!" They crashed into two of Madame Gasket's sweepers. Bigweld popped off the magnet and went flying right through the Chop Shop doors!

CHAPTER TEN

Rusties to the Rescue!

Bigweld found himself stuck in a cauldron hanging from the ceiling. His was just one of a whole row of cauldrons moving slowly toward Madame Gasket's grinder. Flames leapt out of the grinder each time a cauldron tipped its contents into it.

Bigweld was preparing for his doom when all of a sudden the grinder came to an abrupt stop. He looked up and saw Rodney and the Wonderbot wedging a metal rod into the gears.

"Argh! Go after them," Madame Gasket ordered her minions. They tried to tackle Rodney and Bigweld, but the Rusties fought them off. They had all arrived on the scene upgraded to look like a motley mix of superheroes.

"Who are you losers, anyway?" asked Madame Gasket.

"We've come to rescue our friends, you evil bag of bolts!" cried Fender.

But then a buzzer sounded and the sweeper bay doors opened wide. A fleet of brand-new high-end sweepers roared through, with Ratchet driving the one in the lead. The Rusties were outnumbered!

Kablam! A big chunk of wall came crashing down behind them. They turned to see Piper stepping through the opening. "Did I miss the butt-whupping?" she asked.

Hundreds of outmodes followed her in, spinning their wrenches, ready to fight. Aunt Fan brought in the backup, carrying more fighters in her fanny. All the bots Rodney had helped were now here to help him.

The minions and outmodes surged toward each other. The clang of metal parts filled the air.

Aunt Fan tried to whack the enemy with her wooden spoon, but her fanny did most of the fighting.

In the midst of the fighting, Madame Gasket yanked on the metal rod that had jammed the gears. She

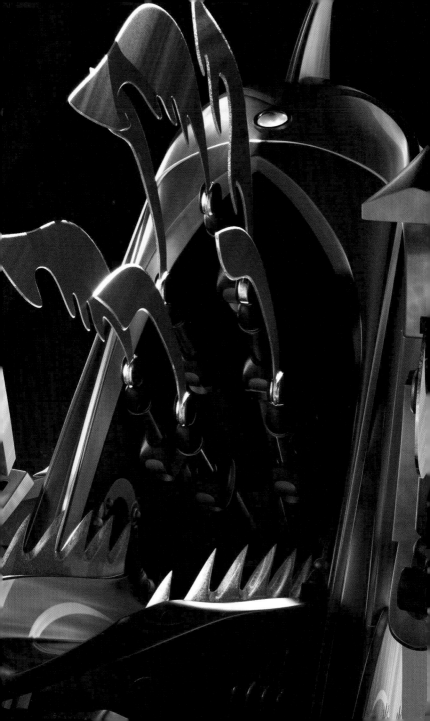

laughed as Bigweld's cauldron moved toward the fiery grinder. Rodney flew up on the Wonderbot to save him. While Rodney was helping Bigweld out of the cauldron, the Wonderbot zoomed in to distract Madame Gasket. Bigweld and Rodney grabbed onto the chain, cut the cauldron free, and were lifted up into the rafters.

From above they could survey the scene. It didn't look good for the Rusties. Ratchet had cornered the Rusties with the sweepers. They had to think fast. Rodney looked around for inspiration. He spotted a big saw blade hanging from an archway directly above him. Bigweld's eyes followed Rodney's gaze. "Are you thinking what I'm thinking?" he asked.

"I sure am!" Rodney yelled. With that, Rodney released the saw and the pair went flying through the air toward the sweepers. The blade zipped right past Ratchet—a near miss! But Rodney and Bigweld were headed somewhere more important. They crashed into the first sweeper, knocking it into the sweeper next to it. Then, like Bigweld's dominoes, all of the huge

CHAPTER ELEVEN

Homecoming Hero

Rodney couldn't wait to get home to Rivet Town to see his mom and dad.

"Herb! Come outside! Hurry!" Rodney's mom said as she burst through the restaurant doors.

Mr. Copperbottom was afraid something bad had happened to his son. But before he could follow his wife outside, Mr. Gunk stormed in. "Where are you going? What about the dishes?"

There was only one thing to do. After shoving his dishwashing unit onto Mr. Gunk, Herb Copperbottom finally made it out of the restaurant.

He was astonished. The whole town had gathered to welcome Rodney home. A camera bot snapped his photo. When his eyes had recovered from the flash, Mr. Copperbottom saw Bigweld standing right before him.

Bigweld shook Mr. Copperbottom's hand. "I came all this way to tell you that your son, Rodney, is now my right-hand bot and my eventual successor!"

The crowd cheered.

Rodney's mom rushed over and gave Rodney and his dad big hugs.

"Dad," declared Rodney, "if not for you, this never would've happened. I'd still be back in my room, day-dreaming."

Mrs. Copperbottom dabbed a tear from her eye.

"You told me to go after my dream," Rodney continued. "Now I want your dream to come true." He presented his dad with a fancy new musical upgrade, just like he had always wanted. Mr. Copperbottom was touched. He honked out a few notes, and soon everyone joined in, in a crazy victory song!

Rodney had proven that you really can shine no matter what you were made of.